X084362

The item should be returned or renewed by the last date stamped below.

Dylid dychwelyd neu adnewyddu'r eitem erbyn y dyddiad olaf sydd wedi'i stampio isod.

D1313120

To renew visit / Adnewyddwch ar
www.newport.gov.uk/libraries

Maverick
Chapter Readers

'Monster Cuts'
An original concept by W. G. White
© W. G. White 2021

Illustrated by Lilia Miceli

Published by MAVERICK ARTS PUBLISHING LTD

Studio 11, City Business Centre, 6 Brighton Road,

Horsham, West Sussex, RH13 5BB

© Maverick Arts Publishing Limited November 2021

+44 (0)1403 256941

A CIP catalogue record for this book is available at the British Library.

ISBN 978-1-84886-839-7

www.maverickbooks.co.uk

This book is rated as: Lime Band (Guided Reading)

Monster Cuts

Written by
W. G. White

Illustrated by
Lilia Miceli

Chapter 1

At the end of a windy driveway, under a tall mountain and surrounded by snowy trees, was Louise's new house. But Louise wasn't happy or even a little excited. Louise didn't think there was anything wrong with her *old* house. She loved her old house. It wasn't big or fancy, but it was home.

"What do you think?" asked Mum.

"I want to go home," replied Louise.

"We are home, love!"

Louise watched as Mum moved boxes. Instead of helping, she crossed her arms and stomped her feet. This *wasn't* home. How would the postman know where to deliver her letters? And her friends! They were all so far away now. It wasn't fair!

"Come on," Mum said, taking Louise's hand. "Let's see our new salon!"

Not far from the new house was the longest high street Louise had ever seen. It had snowy forests on either side of it, and lots of people rushing up and down. Mum led Louise all the way to the bottom of the street.

"Ta-da!" said Mum, pointing to a tiny hair salon with old walls. It looked like it'd been empty for years. "It needs a name, yes. But we'll come up with something amazing."

Louise crossed her arms and huffed. She didn't care! She just wanted to go home!

Chapter 2

One week later, Louise hadn't stopped frowning. She'd frowned through her lessons at her new school. She'd frowned through meal times and even her favourite TV shows.

Mum sighed as she counted out the salon's daily earnings. "Business is slow..."

Louise wanted to hug her mum, but didn't. She was still cross. Instead, Louise snatched her coat and stormed off, out of the house. She walked into the nearby forests, listening to the snow crunch beneath her feet.

"Stupid house," she muttered to herself. "Stupid salon." She stopped in her tracks. A small, snow-covered tree was in her way. "Stupid tree!" She kicked the tree which, surprisingly, *yelped.*

"Ouch!" exclaimed the tree. It hopped on one leg, snow falling from its fur.

Leg? Trees don't have legs. Or fur... They have trunks. And leaves!

"Oh dear," said Louise. She'd not kicked a tree... she'd kicked a yeti.

"*Oh dear?!*" howled the yeti. "You kicked me!"

"Sorry... I thought you were a tree."

"Trees don't like to be kicked either, you mean little human. Oh, gosh... Look, I'm really very sorry, but I'm going to have to eat you now."

"Eat me?" Louise backed away from the yeti. "But why? I said I was sorry!"

"I don't like it either but that's just the way it is. Now, stay still. I've not had human before and I'm told you taste worse if you run."

Chapter 3

Louise did not stay still. She ran fast and she ran far. The yeti bumbled after her. He yelped, grumbled, and tutted as he bumped into trees and tripped over roots.

"Aha! I've got you!" shouted the yeti.

He didn't have her. Not even close.

Louise stopped running and turned to look at the yeti. He was gnawing on a skinny tree.

She couldn't help but laugh. He didn't seem so scary anymore.

"You taste horrible," he said in disgust. "Like a tree."

"Because that *is* a tree." Louise giggled. Then she felt sorry for the yeti. His fur was ruffled from bumping into trees, and his ice-blue eyes were

barely visible beneath his long, tangled fringe.

He was panting too. All that fur must have been

terribly hot.

"I know that," he said, releasing the tree. "I

was just... sharpening my teeth."

"You can't see very well, can you?" Louise

asked. "And you're much too warm."

"How dare you!" exclaimed the yeti. "My eyesight's perfect."

Louise would have believed him if he wasn't speaking to a rock.

"How about a deal?" asked Louise. "You promise not to eat me, and my mum will cut your hair. You'll be able to see again!"

The yeti thought for a moment. "Can I eat your mum?"

"No!"

"Fine! Didn't wanna eat her anyway... I accept your deal." He trudged towards her and stuck out a huge hand. "Call me Garrrath."

Louise accepted the hand and shook it. "I'm Louise. Nice to meet you."

Chapter 4

Louise snuck Garrath down the high street.

She tried to keep the yeti hidden, knowing most

people would probably be

scared of him.

They soon arrived at Mum's salon. The door's bell dinged as an old woman hurried outside. She had the best mohawk Louise had ever seen. Mum was *really* good at mohawks.

"I wanted a perm!" shouted the woman, who spotted Garrrath as she ran out of the shop.

"M-M-M-Monster!"

she screeched, terror painted on her face.

The woman fled and Louise hurried Garrrath inside, out of sight. She made sure to close the curtains behind her.

"She said she wanted *something different,*" Mum muttered as she swept up hair clippings. "A mohawk's different!" She froze when she spotted Garrrath. "Louise... who's this?"

"Hello," said Garrrath, though he was talking to a coat rack. "One haircut please."

"This is Garrrath, he's a yeti," explained Louise. "He promised not to eat me and I promised him a haircut."

"Well that... makes perfect sense..." Mum blinked, shook herself and prepared her equipment as Louise guided Garrrath into the chair.

"I wasn't actually going to eat you," said Garrrath to Louise as Mum got to work with her scissors. "Maybe just an arm or two. I just don't like being kicked. Sorry I chased you."

Mum snipped and combed, cut and razored. She was like a hairdressing wizard as she styled Garrrath's long, snowy fur into an awesome quiff.

It reminded Louise of Elvis Presley's hair, only bigger.

"Hold on," said Mum. She rushed into a cupboard and dug out a pair of extra large skinny jeans and a waistcoat, which Garrrath squeezed himself into. "Those will finish you off."

"Wowza!" Garrrath roared with excitement. He looked more or less like a hairy human. He looked like a rock star. "I *have* to tell everyone!" He rushed to the door and threw it open. "I'll bring my entire clan back tomorrow, just you see!"

Chapter 5

The next day came quickly and Louise found herself excited to visit the salon. She couldn't wait to meet Garrrath's family and see what Mum would do with their hair. Perhaps living here wouldn't be so bad after all.

The salon had only been open for five minutes when there was a forceful knock on the door.

"I'll get it!" Louise declared as she rushed to open the door. But instead of masses of white fur ready for snipping, Louise saw only two tidy, black suits.

"Are you the owner of this haircutting business?" said one of the suit-wearing people. He was a tall, skinny man with not a single hair on his head.

"Yes, that would be me," Mum said. "What's wrong?"

In perfect unison the suit-wearing-people whipped out ID badges and flashed them in Mum's face.

"Agent Mary M. Alice," said the second suit-wearing-person. She was just as tall and skinny as her friend, and didn't have much more hair. "This is my partner, Agent David D. Light. We're here on urgent MI0 business, responding to reports of supernatural sightings. Have you seen anything suspicious, spooky, or spectacular recently?"

Oh no! thought Louise. *They're here for Garrrath!*

"MI0?" said Mum. "Like MI5? Spies and stuff?"

"That's top secret," replied Agent D. Light.

"We've not seen anything suspicious," said Louise, and Mum agreed.

The agents looked at each other and sighed.

"We'll be back for a proper search of local businesses at noon when we have our equipment," said Agent M. Alice. "Just to be sure."

When the MI0 agents left, Louise rushed into the forests, searching for Garrrath. She needed to warn him so he and his family would be safe! But she couldn't find him anywhere, no matter how hard she looked. Disappointed, she returned to the salon and waited.

Chapter 6

At 11:57 am, there was still no sign of Garrrath or his family. The MIO agents would arrive at noon. What if the yetis turned up then? The agents would take them away!

At 11:58 am, Louise's pacing was starting to make Mum dizzy. At 11:59 am, the salon's door dinged. In walked Garrrath, still trendy in his new clothes and massive quiff.

Behind him was a group of terribly hairy yetis.

"Hello!" Garrrath shouted with a wave. "I'm back with my—"

"**There's no time!**" declared Louise as she rushed the yetis through the back room door. There were five of them in total, all different shapes and sizes, but all covered in snowy white fur.

At 12:00 pm, a big black truck rolled into town. It stopped at the top of the high street and a gang of suit-wearing agents hopped out, setting up a perimeter across the whole of the high street.

Then, they started invading shops with all

sorts of crazy-looking gadgets and gizmos.

"They're here!" said Louise. "We've got to

get cutting, Mum!"

"Who's here?" asked Garrrath.

"MIO! They're looking for anything suspicious,

spooky, or spectacular."

"But we're spooky *and* spectacular!" shouted one of the yetis. There was panic amongst the monster folk and they looked like they were ready to run away. If they did, they would surely be caught by MIO.

"What are we going to do?" Garrrath wailed.

"Don't worry, we can hide you in plain sight," said Mum. She gave her scissors a good snip and grinned. "Who's first?"

Chapter 7

Mum gave Cousin Barrrt a mohawk and Louise

dressed him in a skull t-shirt and ripped jeans.

Sister Roaria got a stylish bob and a lovely dress.

Grandpa Grumpy wanted a bald head, a bushy

beard, and a comfy onesie, whilst Mother Furlicity

chose a neat bun and a warm winter shawl.

One by one, Mum and Louise transformed the

yetis from monsters to people.

The floor was swimming in fur and it took Louise and Mum ages to sweep it all away.

But whilst Mum and Louise worked, the MIO agents steadily grew closer and closer.

Mum snipped the final hair on the final yeti just as the door's bell chimed. In walked Agents D. Light and M. Alice. They wore sunglasses and black suits as they looked the shop up and down.

"Do not be alarmed," Agent D. Light said as he pulled a computer thingy out of his jacket. "We're here to search for dangerous creatures. Go about your regular business."

"There aren't any monsters here so you're wasting your time," said Louise. She only hoped she and Mum had done a good enough job disguising the yetis.

The agents moved through the shop, inspecting every surface and corner with their

weird devices. They left no stone unturned and soon began paying closer attention to the yetis.

"Your customers are very hairy," remarked Agent M. Alice.

"Of course they are," replied Louise. "It's a salon."

"And awfully tall..."

"It's the forest air," said Mum. "Very good for your growth."

Agent D. Light crossed his arms and said, "They smell like woodland beasts."

The yetis pretended to be outraged by the comment, and Louise joined them. "That's a very rude thing to say," she declared. "You should say you're sorry right away!"

Agent M. Alice's radio crackled and a voice said, *"Come in all agents. We've got a possible Code Dracula at the Steak House. All agents to the Steak House. Bring garlic."*

"Copy that. We're on our way," said M. Alice into her radio. The MIO agents rushed to the door without another word and vanished up the street.

Chapter 8

MIO didn't find a vampire in the Steak House, only an old man with pointy dentures. They packed up their equipment and left not long after, declaring a false alarm and that the town was monster-free.

Louise let out a sigh of relief. Garrrath and his family were safe, styled, and looking good.

They vanished back into the forests, promising to spread the word of Mum's amazing salon.

A week later and the salon was booming. Everyone wanted Mum's crazy haircuts and Louise's cool fashion advice. Louise and Mum decided on the salon's name together and when the sign arrived they couldn't stop smiling.

"It's a good name, love," said Mum.

"Monster Cuts," read Louise with a grin.

It felt like more than a good name.

It felt like home.

Discussion Points

1. What did Louise think Garrrath was when she first met him?

2. Why does Louise feel sorry for Garrath?

a) Because he lives in the woods

b) Because he likes eating trees

c) Because he gets very hot and can't see well

3. What was your favourite part of the story?

4. How do Louise and Mum save the yetis?

5. Why do you think MIO were looking for anything suspicious, spooky, or spectacular?

6. Who was your favourite character and why?

7. There were moments in the story when Louise had to deal with **change**. Where do you think the story shows this most?

8. What do you think happens after the end of the story?

Book Bands for Guided Reading

The Institute of Education book banding system is a scale of colours that reflects the various levels of reading difficulty. The bands are assigned by taking into account the content, the language style, the layout and phonics. Word, phrase and sentence level work is also taken into consideration.

The Maverick Readers Scheme is a bright, attractive range of books covering the pink to grey bands. All of these books have been book banded for guided reading to the industry standard and edited by a leading educational consultant.

To view the whole Maverick Readers scheme, visit our website at
www.maverickearlyreaders.com

Or scan the QR code to view our scheme instantly!

Pink

Red

Yellow

Blue

Green

Orange

Turquoise

Purple

Gold

White

Lime

Brown

Grey

Maverick Chapter Readers
(From Lime to Grey Band)